Introducing Pop Monsters...

Deep in the heart of the Pacific Northwest there lives a furry band of critters that come in all shapes and sizes. In that wooded glen, among the misty meadows and mossy-bearded trees, they share fun and adventure in a magical place called Wetmore Forest.

STERLING CHILDREN'S BOOKS
New York

An Imprint of Sterling Publishing Co., Inc.
1166 Avenue of the Americas
New York, NY 10036

ISBN 978-1-4549-3492-9

For information about custom editions, special sales, and premium and corporate purchases, please contact Sterling Special Sales at 800-805-5489 or specialsales@sterlingpublishing.com.

Manufactured in China
Lot #: .
2 4 6 8 10 9 7 5 3 1
03/19

sterlingpublishing.com

PICKLEZ
GETS LUNCH

A
WETMORE FOREST
STORY

By Randy Harvey and Sean Wilkinson
Illustrated by John Skewes

STERLING CHILDREN'S BOOKS
New York

One day in Wetmore Forest, Picklez was walking along when he heard a terrible growling noise. At first he was scared. Then he realized it was just his stomach telling him it was time for lunch. That's when he spied a towering Mushberry bush, its branches dripping with delicious Mushberries.

Of all the wonderful things to eat in Wetmore forest,

thought Picklez, *Mushberries are my very favorite!*

Excited, he hurried up the trail.

But as he got closer, he saw that someone else had the same idea.

An enormous horned Hoppnopper was feasting on the bush, using its long snout to happily suck up all the berries within reach.

Picklez watched
as the Hoppnopper
grabbed the bush and

shook
Shook
shook

it . . .

. . . until more berries fell onto the ground.

Picklez ran to scoop up some of the berries, but the mean old Hoppnopper swished him away with its long tail.

No fair, thought Picklez. *Some of us just have regular snouts that can't reach the high branches!*

Then, Picklez had an idea. Maybe he could trick the Hoppnopper into shaking loose some berries for him!

He waited until the Hoppnopper drifted off for its afternoon nap.

Then Picklez crept up close to the sleeping beast and began to tickle its snout with a Squim-hawk feather.

The Hoppnopper twitched. It twittered. Then it

Sneezed a giant sneeze.

But it did not wake up.

"Huh," huffed Picklez.

You might think that Picklez would have given up by now. But that just wasn't his style. Plus, he was really hungry. He searched all around for things that made noise to wake the sleeping Hoppnopper.

He found **splats** …

… and **shrieks** …

… and **pops!**

But nothing seemed to work.

Hmmm. Maybe I've been going about this all wrong, thought Picklez as he picked up a smooth little pebble from the ground.

Placing the pebble into the end of a hollow reed, Picklez took cover behind a large rock. He aimed the reed at the sleeping Hoppnopper, drew a deep breath, and blew as hard as he could. The pebble shot out of the reed and hit the snoozing beast right . . . on . . . the rump!

Now **THAT** got its attention!

Confused, the Hoppnopper leapt to its feet,
running and bucking in little circles.
Then it saw Picklez.

Picklez ran. The Hoppnopper chased him . . .

. . . and chased him . . .

. . . and chased him . . .

. . . but that mean Hoppnopper was never going to catch Picklez. Everybody knew Picklez was the fastest monster in all of Wetmore Forest.

Finally, after he had the Hoppnopper good and worn out, Picklez skidded to a stop behind the trunk of the Mushberry bush. He smiled to himself.

The Hoppnopper was so mad that it wasn't looking
where it was going. It smashed into the Mushberry
bush at full force, shaking it so hard all the remaining
berries came raining down!

The Hoppnopper turned around to face Picklez. It opened its mouth, and Picklez braced himself for a giant ROAR. But instead, the Hoppnopper . . .

. . . gave an amused SNORT. Then he and Picklez began

gobbling up the delicious Mushberries together.

Their tummies full and their mouths stained with berries, the new friends lay back against the base of the Mushberry bush.

Picklez held the last remaining berry between his fingers. *Better savor it*, he thought, and tossed the berry into the air.

Turns out, Hoppnoppers are pretty fast, too.

Collect all of the
WETMORE FOREST
Adventures.

Available now:

Coming Soon!